WISHBONE™'s Tales of a Pup

Wishbone and the Glass Slipper

A. D. Francis

Illustrated by Kathryn Yingling

Inspired by Cinderella

Little Red Chair Books™
A Division of Lyrick Publishing™

WISHBONE™
created by Rick Duffield

This book is a work of fiction. The characters, incidents, and dialogues are products of the author's imagination and are not to be construed as real. Any resemblance to actual events or persons, living or dead, is entirely coincidental.

Little Red Chair Books™, A Division of **Lyrick Publishing**™
300 E. Bethany Drive, Allen, Texas 75002

© 2000 Big Feats Entertainment, L.P. All rights reserved. **WISHBONE** and the **Wishbone** portrait and Big Feats! Entertainment logos are trademarks and service marks of Big Feats Entertainment, L.P. Little Red Chair Books and Lyrick Publishing are trademarks and service marks of Lyrick Studios, Inc. WISHBONE and the Wishbone portrait and the Big Feats! Entertainment logos, and Lyrick Publishing are Reg. U.S. Pat. & Tm. Off.

All rights reserved. No part of this book may be used or reproduced in any manner whatsoever without written permission of the publisher, except in the case of brief quotations embodied in critical articles and reviews. For information address **Lyrick Publishing**™, 300 E. Bethany Drive, Allen, Texas, 75002. Produced by By George Productions, Inc.

Library of Congress Catalog Card Number: 00-103254

ISBN: 1-58668-001-3

First printing: July 2000

10 9 8 7 6 5 4 3 2

Printed in the United States of America

A NOTE TO FAMILIES

As a star on PBS, and in Adventure and Mystery books for older readers, Wishbone™ has introduced millions of children to classic stories.

Now, everybody's favorite pooch brings classic tales to *first readers,* too! In Wishbone's Tales of a Pup timeless fantasies feature Wishbone still in his spunky puppy years.

Wishbone's Tales of a Pup are carefully written with young readers in mind. The stories are exciting, the text is just challenging enough to keep them growing, and the illustrations enhance the fun.

Whether your own young pup is reading this book to you, or is still enjoying having you read aloud, here are some ways to keep reading a part of your family activities:

● Create a special place at home for reading. A comfortable nook or chair can become a magic carpet to other worlds.
● Let your children see you reading! They will see the importance you place on it and make it a habit of their own.
● Ask them about what they've read. Talking about it strengthens their storytelling skills and reinforces reading comprehension.
● Give them the gift of a library card, and visit your library often! Most libraries have special children's programs, and the staff can match your child's interests with a wide range of books.

Enjoy this tale-wagging series!

Little Red Chair Books™

Helllooo!

Yes, it's me, Wishbone!
You caught me chewing on
a slipper. It's good to have a
slipper around. And not just
because they're yummy and
fun to fetch. Slippers can
come in handy. Just ask my
good friend, Cinderpup.
You know his story, don't
you? You don't? Then by all
means grab a slipper and
get comfortable.

Chapter One

The whole thing started once upon a time, when there lived a fine gentleman and his handsome son, Pup.

Pup and his father were happy together. During the day, they played fetch and took long walks in the garden. At night they dined on juicy steaks. After burying the bones, Pup curled up in his warm bed and dreamed of the next day.

One day, Pup's dad came
home with a surprise.

"Meet your new stepmother
and stepbrothers," he told Pup.

Pup made the best of his new
family. But he missed his time
alone with his dad. Then, sadly
and suddenly, Pup's father died.

And right away, everything changed.

While her lazy sons stayed in bed or laid around playing games, Pup's stepmother put him to work. From morning to night, he scrubbed floors and washed dishes. He worked like . . . well, like a dog. He had no time for walks in the garden. And he never had time to chew a slipper or fetch things for fun.

Pup did not get to sleep
in a warm bed. His stepmother
made him sleep on a pile
of straw.

Pup tried to ignore the fact
that his family treated him like
a servant. He turned away when
his mean stepbrothers called
him "Cinderpup." It wasn't his

fault he was always covered in cinders from the fireplace!

Pup worked hard. And when his work was done, he curled up near the chimney where it was nice and warm. He dreamed of long walks, games of fetch, and juicy steaks.

Chapter Two

Then one bright morning, something special came in the mail. It was an invitation to a ball. The dance would be held at the castle that very evening!

As he carried the mail inside, Cinderpup wagged his tail excitedly. The castle! A princess!

Cinderpup's stepbrothers jumped up and down.

There was no time to lose! Right away, they put Cinderpup to work.

"Sew this button on my red velvet suit," one stepbrother ordered Cinderpup.

"No! First iron the ruffles on my white shirt," the other commanded.

But Cinderpup was also excited. "I need to get ready, too," he told them.

"You?!" The stepbrothers laughed.

"Why not me?" Cinderpup asked, pricking his ears.

"For one thing, you're dirty," said the first stepbrother.

"And you have nothing to wear," the second one added.

Cinderpup looked down at his ragged, sooty clothes. His tail hung between his legs. "I guess you are right," he sighed.

"Of course they are!" his stepmother told him.

Chapter Three

That night, Cinderpup waved goodbye to his family as they left for the ball. Then he curled up on his pile of straw and rested his head on his paws. "I wish . . . I wish . . ." he muttered.

"What do you wish?" a friendly voice asked.

Cinderpup looked up. It was a fairy godmother!

Cinderpup leapt to his feet. "I wish I could go to the ball," he told her. "To see the beautiful castle and meet the princess."

"And so you shall!" the fairy

godmother replied.

"But how?" asked Cinderpup.
He held up his dirty paws.
"I have no—"

"Tut-tut," his fairy godmother
shushed him. "Just run into the
garden and fetch me a pumpkin."

Cinderpup did not know how a
pumpkin could help him go to the
ball. But he did as he was told.

Cinderpup hurried to the garden. He picked the finest, orangest pumpkin he could find. His fairy godmother tapped it lightly with her wand. In an instant, the pumpkin turned into a fancy golden coach! And that wasn't all. Six mice from the kitchen pantry became six dapple-gray horses. A rat from the barn became a black-whiskered coachman.

And last but not least, six lizards from behind the well became six footmen.

Cinderpup was amazed —and very pleased!

"Now off you go!" said the fairy godmother.

Cinderpup cocked his head. He didn't want to seem ungrateful, but . . . "What about my clothes?" he asked.

"Oh, of course!" The fairy godmother smiled and waved her magic wand.

Through a shower of fairy dust, Cinderpup looked down at his fancy new suit. It was made of bright, soft silk. And he wore beautiful buckled glass slippers, fit for a king.

Cinderpup was so happy he could have licked his fairy godmother. "How can I ever thank you?" he asked.

"Just have a wonderful time," the fairy godmother said. "But be sure to be home by midnight. One minute more and the coach will turn back into a pumpkin.

The horses will be mice. The coachman will be a rat. The footmen will be lizards. And your clothes will be just as ragged as they were before."

"I promise," Cinderpup said with a wag of his tail. Then he jumped into his golden coach and sped off to the ball.

Chapter Four

The moment Cinderpup arrived at the castle, a buzz went through the crowd.

"Who is that handsome stranger?" everyone asked. "Such grand clothes! And those slippers!"

Even Cinderpup's stepbrothers thought the handsome stranger was a prince from a far off land. They had no idea at all he was really Cinderpup!

The princess thought Cinderpup was the handsomest guest at the ball. She had a special place set for him at her table. She danced every dance with him. In fact, she did not leave Cinderpup's side all evening.

Cinderpup loved every minute—and every juicy steak and chop. He was so excited, he did a little flip—right in the middle of the dance floor. The princess laughed and clapped. It was a wonderful night. So wonderful that Cinderpup completely forgot the time . . .

The next thing Cinderpup
knew, the clock in the castle
tower was striking midnight.

Uh-oh! Cinderpup suddenly
dropped the tasty sausage he
had been nibbling.

"Sorry, Princess," he said as he
raced for the door. "Gotta go!"

Stunned, the princess chased after him.

"Wait!" she called. "I don't know your name!"

But Cinderpup did not wait. He could not let the princess see him wearing rags!

When the princess reached the street, her prince was gone. On the cobblestones, she saw only a big orange pumpkin . . . and a shiny glass slipper.

The princess recognized the slipper at once. It belonged to her prince. But how would she ever find him again?

Chapter Five

The very next morning, Cinderpup fetched the mail and found a proclamation. It said that the princess would stop at nothing to find the owner of the glass slipper. Her servant would visit each and every house in the kingdom. And every member of

every household would be asked to try on the glass slipper.

Cinderpup was thrilled. The princess was looking for him! Soon his stepbrothers and stepmother would know that *he* was the handsome stranger at the ball.

But Cinderpup's stepmother had other plans.

"Get upstairs and clean the attic," she ordered. "I don't want to see you again until it is spick and span."

Cinderpup groaned. The attic was a mess! How could he clean it before the royal servant arrived?

Still, Cinderpup did not argue. He took the mop and pail and hurried up the stairs.

Cinderpup worked as fast as he could. He dusted and swept and mopped. As soon as he was finished, he raced down the stairs.

His stepbrothers were just trying on the slipper when he came into the parlor. They each tried desperately to squeeze a foot into the tiny slipper. But it was like trying to squeeze a Saint Bernard into a Chihuahua's sweater.

Then the servant stood up to leave. Cinderpup stopped him just in time. "May I try?" he asked politely.

Cinderpup's stepmother glared at him. His stepbrothers roared with laughter. "You!" they all exclaimed.

But the servant had orders to let everyone try. Even a dirty stepchild. He knelt down in front of Cinderpup—and Cinderpup smiled as his paw slid easily into the slipper.

Cinderpup's family could not

believe it. The puppy they had all
made fun of and ordered around
was the same handsome stranger
they had seen at the ball!

To Cinderpup's surprise, they
fell to their knees and begged
him to forgive them. And
because he was as kind as he
was handsome, Cinderpup did.

In fact, Cinderpup even let his family live with him in the royal castle. Cinderpup's dreams had come true. He was happy, and he wanted everyone else to be happy, too.

And so for as long as there were royal balls to chase and grand gardens to run through, they all lived together, happily ever after.

So you see, it's always good to have a slipper handy! Take it from Cinderpup and Wishbone.

Now, if you'll excuse me, I've got some serious chewing to do.

9 781586 680015

ISBN 1-58668-001-3